Boy King

For Michael and Harry

Boy King

David Belbin

A & C Black • London

TUDOR FLASHBACKS
Boy King • David Belbin
Robbers on the Road • Melvin Burgess
The Eyes of Doctor Dee • Maggie Pearson
Gunner's Boy • Ann Turnbull

also available:
WORLD WAR II FLASHBACKS
The Right Moment • David Belbin
Final Victory • Herbie Brennan
Blitz Boys • Linda Newbery
Blood and Ice • Neil Tonge

VICTORIAN FLASHBACKS
Soldier's Son • Garry Kilworth
A Slip in Time • Maggie Pearson
Out of the Shadow • Margaret Nash
The Voyage of the Silver Bream • Theresa Tomlinson

First paperback edition 2003
First published in hardback 2002
by A & C Black (Publishers) Ltd
37 Soho Square, London, W1D 3QZ
www.acblack.com

Text copyright © 2002 David Belbin

ISBN 0-7136-6318-9

A CIP catalogue record for this book is available
from the British Library.

Printed and bound in Great Britain by
Creative Print & Design (Wales), Ebbw Vale

Contents

Part One: 1548

1 ❧ The King is Dead

'It must be bad news, Edward,' my sister said. 'Why else would they have brought you all this way?'

We were talking in whispers while waiting for my uncle to join us.

'When did you last see the King?' I asked Elizabeth.

'Weeks ago.'

'Me too,' I admitted. I wasn't allowed to visit the King because London was so disease-ridden. Half the children there die before they're sixteen. I was the King's only male child, the heir to the throne. My life must never be put at risk.

'He looked awful last time he came to Hampton Court,' I said.

'The end must be close,' Elizabeth replied, squeezing my hand. 'That's why you've been getting all those extra lessons.'

When I last saw him, my father could hardly get on a horse, he weighed so much. He'd had a bad leg for two years and his sight was going. He bought pairs of glasses ten at a time and left them all over every one of his palaces. Some days, I'd heard, he didn't even get dressed. He had to be carried around in a fancy chair on wooden poles. They called it The King's Machine.

'If he's dead...' Elizabeth began to speak, but I interrupted.

'He's not dead. He might be dying but he won't be dead for ages.'

'If he's dead, you don't have to do what anybody says. You'll be the king.'

We were standing in the Presence Chamber, which was cold and draughty, but that wasn't why I shivered.

'I'll do whatever the King tells me to do,' I told my sister.

'You'll be the king,' Elizabeth repeated, as if I hadn't got the point. 'You won't have to do what anybody else tells you to.'

Then Uncle Edward joined us. He knelt before me and I knew what was coming next. I was nine years old. Elizabeth was just thirteen.

Afterwards, Elizabeth and I hugged each other and we both cried, but only for a while. The news was not expected, but hardly a surprise. A new feeling came over me. It wasn't grief, but something bigger, something I had not felt before.

Uncle Edward knelt and pledged his loyalty to me as his king. Then – slowly, clearly, because it was so important – he explained who was next in line to the throne. Our older sister Mary (daughter of my father's first wife) would become queen should I die without an heir. After her, Elizabeth. My sisters shouldn't get their hopes up, I thought. Women only rule if there is no male directly in line to the throne. There hasn't been a queen without a king since Boudicca in the first century.

Next morning, Uncle Edward and I set off on horseback for London. Once we were under way, he explained that my father's death had not yet been announced.

'There are those who oppose you coming to the throne,' he said. 'We won't give them the chance to do anything about it...'

He was talking about the Catholics. Despite setting up the Church of England, my father stayed a kind of Catholic – it was the faith of his childhood, after all. Most people in England still wanted to be Catholics. The reformers – or Protestants – were mainly to be found in London, especially at court. My stepmother, Queen Catherine, was a Protestant.

So were both of my uncles. Me, too. But the Catholics were almost as strong.

The ride took four hours and there was no trouble on the way. When we got to Whitehall, trumpets sounded.

'Are they for me?' I asked Uncle Edward.

'No, for your father. It's dinner time.'

The trumpets sounded three times a day, announcing meals being taken to the King. My father had not been moved since his death. As far as people knew, Henry VIII was alive and well and waiting for his dinner.

'I want to see him,' I begged.

'No. You must go straight to the Tower. It's the tradition.'

I started to feel the chill of the cold January day. For there was another tradition at the Tower of London. It was where Elizabeth's mother, Ann Boleyn, was beheaded. Her, and a thousand others.

As we rode on, Uncle Edward explained how things would work from now on. My father had appointed a Council to rule the country until I came of age. I knew this already. Uncle Edward and my other uncle, Thomas Seymour, were both on it. So was John Dudley, the great general. The Council felt

that there should be one 'special man' in charge, a
Lord Protector.

'And who will that be?' I asked, for I hadn't
expected this.

Uncle Edward, with his fair hair, long beard and
friendly, wise smile, used his most humble voice.
'Who would you suggest?'

There was only one answer I could give. Uncle
Edward should become the Lord Protector of
England, Wales and Ireland.

'Whatever they call me,' my uncle insisted, 'you
are absolute king. You are as powerful at nine as you
will be at nineteen or ninety. I am your servant.'

There have been many other young kings. I have
good reason to know my history. But none was as
powerful as I became that afternoon. The thought
terrified me.

2 ❧ Long Live the King

I smelt them before I heard them. There was a dense, earthy smell which I'd been protected from all my life. It was the stench of people squashed together, all of their essences and odours mingling with the smoky air. Then, as we got nearer to the Tower, the low roar of the crowd started to reach my ears. Shouted conversations and laughter rang out above the persistent rumble, the echoing, ominous sound of expectation.

I saw them at the same time as they saw me. More people than I had ever seen in my life before. The streets were full. Every window and doorway was crammed with watchers. A mighty roar went up as my uncle and I – in all our finery – rode into view. Despite the crush, people made way for us. Uncle Edward turned and said something to me, but I couldn't make out his words above the endless shouts of affection, of celebration. The news of my father's death had only just got out. The city was supposed to be in mourning. They should have been wailing, 'The King is dead!' Instead they were calling out, 'Long live the King!'

As soon as we arrived inside the Tower, Archbishop Cranmer and the lords of the Council knelt before me.

'I was with the King when he died,' the Archbishop told me. 'He was at peace.'

Awkwardly, I motioned the lords to rise. They led me into the Presence Chamber of the Tower. It had been newly hung with cloth made of gold. The lords made short speeches, each pledging loyalty to me. I tried hard to listen, to be as regal as it's possible for a nine-year-old boy to be, but I was tired and my clothes were dusty from the journey. I was glad to escape to my rooms to change. Outside, cannons blasted away, even though I had yet to be officially proclaimed king. It was three o'clock in the morning before I sat down with the Council. I had hardly slept for two days, yet I was so excited that I was beyond tiredness. Archbishop Cranmer got down to business straight away. He told me that with sixteen members on the Council they felt the need for one man to be their leader.

'Are you willing for your uncle Edward Seymour to be proclaimed Lord Protector of the realm and governor of your person during your minority?'

I hadn't discussed that last bit with Uncle Edward, but I told the Archbishop that I was willing anyway. Each Council member then kissed my hand, Uncle Edward going first.

They all said, 'God save Your Grace!'

When it was Uncle Thomas's turn, he winked at me. After they were all done, Uncle Edward stepped forward and spoke to the Council.

'With your help,' he said, 'I will do my duty.'

The lords of the Council swore allegiance. First to Uncle Edward, the new Lord Protector. Then to me.

Stories are told about my father's funeral: how it took sixteen yeomen of the guard to lift his heavy coffin, how his grave clothes burst open, dripping blood. Don't ask me if they're true. I wasn't there. I was busy in the Tower, preparing for my coronation. My tutor, John Cheke, helped me reply to letters of condolence.

Next day I dressed in a purple velvet robe and a mourning-stole and invested Uncle Thomas as Lord Admiral of the Navy. Then I officially made Uncle Edward (already Lord Protector) the Duke of Somerset. My poor dead mother, Jane Seymour, would have been very proud of her brothers.

Uncle Thomas looked quite like Uncle Edward, with a big beard and a strong face, but he was more handsome. He came to see me often, those days in the Tower – much more often than my other uncle. Uncle Thomas liked to talk of his big plans for the future. Running the navy was just a start for him. Uncle Edward had given his younger brother a lot of land, but that wasn't enough for Thomas. He was going to take more, make more.

'Think of it, nephew,' he said. 'Our family, the Seymours, running the land. Why, ten or eleven years ago, nobody could have dreamt it.'

I loved hearing about Thomas's hopes and plans. He was such an impressive man, tall enough to stand out in any crowd. Uncle Edward was wise and kind, but Uncle Thomas, with his charm and his wonderful voice, was much more exciting to be with.

Yet, while I was a Seymour like my uncles, I was also a Tudor, son of the greatest king my country has ever known. Every night I prayed for the strength to become half as good a monarch as my father. Then I begged God not to let me make a fool of myself at the coronation.

3 ❧ Tightrope

On the day before my coronation, I set out from the Tower to make a ceremonial entry into London. I was dressed in a gown of silver and gold with a belt of rubies, diamonds and pearls, topped by a white velvet cap. When I mounted my horse, under a canopy outside the Tower, six noblemen accompanied me. But because I was small, the crowd couldn't see me, so I rode a few feet ahead of them. Uncle Edward rode to my left, only a little behind.

Behind us were all the people who mattered: courtiers, clergy, ambassadors and the like. They were followed by thousands of men at arms. Streets were roped off. Every building we passed was hung with rich tapestries and golden cloth.

At Fenchurch Street, we paused to listen to a recital of sacred music. Revellers greeted us, their faces red from drinking claret. Children my age performed small plays for the crowds. I tried to watch but their words were drowned out by cries of 'God Save the King!'

It took us more than three hours to reach the Cross in Cheapside. All day, I'd been afraid of showing myself, but by now I was starting to relax. The Mayor of the City knelt before me. He presented me with a purse, so large and so heavy that I could scarcely lift it. In panic I turned to Uncle Edward.

'Why do they give me this?' I asked.

'It is the custom of the City,' he said.

'I can't raise my cap to the crowd if I carry it,' I whispered.

This flustered my uncle. I looked into the bag, which was full of gold coins (a thousand crowns, I learned later – an incredible sum). Uncle Edward motioned me to pass the bag to the Captain of the Guard. The Mayor looked offended, but what else could I do? The bag was too heavy for me to hold.

When we got to St. George's Church, I saw something quite fantastic. A tightrope had been tied to the steeple of the church. It ran to the the Dean's house, where it was fastened to the gate with a heavy anchor. As I approached, a Spanish-looking man appeared at the top of the church battlements. We watched in amazement as he *ran on the rope* from the steeple to the churchyard, where he kissed my foot.

As I gasped, the magical man returned to the tightrope and began to display his amazing abilities – first on one foot then another, balancing on the rope, high in the air. At times he seemed to throw himself off, but never fell. I had never seen anything like it before. Despite Uncle Edward's impatience (we were running very late), I asked the tightrope walker to perform again and again.

The state barge took me up the river to the Palace of Whitehall. While the revels continued, I went to bed – the same bed my father died in. But I was very tired, so it did not bother me. Tomorrow I was to be crowned king.

They woke me at four the next morning. Usually, a coronation would last eleven or twelve hours. Mine, on account of my age, was to be only seven.

A procession formed as we walked up the aisle of Westminster Abbey. Uncle Edward held the crown. Behind him were my school-fellows, each carrying a small part of my regalia. I was glad to see them, but I had no chance to talk to them. As they sat, Archbishop Cranmer made a short speech. I tried to remember everything I had yet to do. Then Uncle Edward led me to the high altar, where the Archbishop was kneeling. Hesitantly, in all my fine clothes, I lay face down on the stairs. The Archbishop prayed aloud. Behind him the choir sang and the organ played *Veni Creator Spiritus*. When it was over, I was taken into a side chapel, where I put on a crimson coat and a cap of gold cloth. Then I was crowned.

'Most dread and royal Sovereign...' Archbishop Cranmer spoke to me alone, but his voice was so loud that the whole Abbey could hear. He repeated my promise to renounce the devil and all his works. He spoke of my father's break with the Roman Catholic Pope. He reminded me that the church was responsible to me, not the other way round. My father had had to swear loyalty to the Pope. I did not. As King of England, I – not the Pope – was God's representative on Earth. When Archbishop Cranmer spoke of the *living god*, I wasn't sure if he meant Almighty God in heaven, or me, a little boy on a throne that was too big for him.

'You are to reward virtue, to revenge sin, to justify the innocent, to relieve the poor, to procure peace, to repress violence, and to execute justice throughout your realms...' Though I was not yet ten years old, the Archbishop crowned me Supreme Head of the Church.

At the banquet, I sat between Uncle Edward and Archbishop Cranmer. After the second course, the king's champion, Sir Robert Dymoke, entered the hall on a horse decked in gold. He rode up to the table, saluted me, then turned to the diners. 'I challenge anyone here present to deny that Edward the Sixth is the rightful heir to throne of England, Ireland and Wales!' With that, he threw down his heavy gauntlet. Nobody picked it up.

That night, no allowances were made for my age, nor did I expect there to be. By the time I left the table, I was exhausted. Still wearing my heavy crown and robes, I had to receive the Ministers of State and foreign ambassadors. The ambassadors were disappointed in me – I was too tired by then to hold a proper conversation in any language.

The rest of the week was taken up by masques and tournaments. Uncle Thomas, the new Lord Admiral, won many jousts. I made sure he saw me clapping loudly. But Uncle Edward, sitting beside me, did not applaud his brother once.

4 🍀 Whipping Boy

All my life I have been used to special treatment, but that was nothing compared with the treatment I received as soon as I became king. At night, for instance, it took ten people to escort me to bed. In near silence. Can you imagine a more boring end to the day? When I wanted my spaniel, Jester, to sleep with me, nobody liked it. But they didn't dare refuse the King, so Jester slept in a basket by the door. At six in the morning, the ritual began all over again, in reverse, with the addition of three chaplains to say prayers with me.

Uncle Thomas visited often. I saw him much more than I saw Uncle Edward. One night he ate with me. It was a simple meal: cold duck, stewed sparrow, larded pheasants, gull and some salad made up the starter. Then we had stork, heron, venison and baked chicken with fritters for the main course. As we ate our dessert of jelly, blancmange and quince pie, I complained of boredom. Uncle Thomas suggested that he find me a friendly servant to make my evenings more entertaining. 'I know just the man,' he said. 'Fowler. Leave it with me.'

The person I trusted most was my tutor. John Cheke, a great scholar. We studied history, geometry and Latin. Most of my reading in English was taken up with the Bible. I worked hard, but when I became bored, John would read poetry, and then we'd talk about it. He was the only one (apart from my uncles) allowed to treat me as an equal. I could be easy with him as I could no longer be with my sisters. Now Elizabeth and Mary were always kneeling and bowing, and sat a long way from me at the dinner table – never really talking with me. Soon Mary moved to her own house.

I had friends, of sorts. They were all older than me. The Council didn't want their boy king playing dangerous sports, but nobody stopped me from running, hunting, shooting at the mark, wrestling, or playing tennis. I was the smallest, though, so I often lost.

One day, I was playing throw and catch with some friends in the library. I missed the ball and it landed on a shelf just out of my reach. Barnaby Fitzpatrick threw down a large book for me to stand on. It was my father's Great Bible. When I refused to stand on it, they all teased me.

'Christ's Passion!' said Barnaby. 'It's only a book.'

'Don't swear at me,' I told him.

'Kings always swear,' Barnaby said. 'Your father was famous for it.'

'Then, by God's Blood, you can get the ball for me!' I swore at him.

They all laughed loudly, not used to hearing me utter an oath. Barnaby reached for the ball. Somebody else put away the Bible.

After that, I swore quite often. It amused me to say *God's Blood!* or *Christ's Passion!* or worse, whenever I felt like it. My new Gentleman Usher, Fowler, laughed quietly when I cursed.

I never swore in front of John Cheke until, one day, we found ourselves discussing the way churches used to be before my father's time. John said there were still churches in England with stained glass windows, showing Christ's crucifixion. Nowadays, all such images were considered blasphemous, Our Lord being too holy to depict.

'God's Blood,' I said. 'Tell me where they are. I'll go and smash them up myself!'

John's warm, freckled face turned cold. 'Who taught you to say those words?' he asked.

'Why, a king may swear. My father...'

'I'm not talking about your father,' he interrupted. 'I'm talking about a ten-year-old boy.'

'Kings always swear, so I've heard.'

'They do not!' John kept at it until I had to admit that one of my friends had put me up to it, though he knew better than to ask me for his name. By the next day, however, he had found it out. When Barnaby Fitzpatrick was brought for punishment, I tried to deny that he was at fault.

'Forget it,' Barnaby whispered. 'I've already confessed.'

I watched as Barnaby removed his shirt, then took six lashes from the whip. I shuddered with each strike. When it was done, I removed my own shirt. John Cheke shook his head.

'I take it you know what a whipping boy is?' he asked.

'I do,' I said, my voice rising in panic. 'But nobody has them any more.'

'The Duke of Richmond had one,' Cheke said, raising the whip again.

This was a name rarely mentioned at court. I wasn't sure why.

'You are the anointed of God,' John went on.

'No man on Earth can punish you. You, in particular, need a whipping boy to pay for your misdeeds. Seeing your friend suffer will be punishment enough for you.'

'No. Stop!' I pleaded.

'I will do it, Your Grace,' Barnaby offered, as the weals on his back grew redder. 'It would be an honour.'

'I can't let you,' I said, stripping off my shirt. 'Punish me, sir. I beg you!'

John put down his whip and told Barnaby to put his shirt back on. 'I think you've both learnt your lesson,' he said. 'Let's hear no more of it.'

From that morning on, Barnaby Fitzpatrick was my best friend.

5 ❧ The Admiral Wants a Wife

'Tell me about the Duke of Richmond,' I whispered in the dark. 'Who was he?'

I was talking to Fowler, my Gentleman Usher. He was a clever man. Uncle Thomas trusted him completely, so I did the same. I had even arranged for Fowler to sleep in the same room as me. No one else was within earshot.

'The Duke of Richmond was your brother, Your Grace,' Fowler whispered. 'He died before you were born – he was only seventeen. His mother was one of the first queen's maids-of-honour.'

'And did he have a whipping boy?' I asked.

'Yes, but he never took a beating. It was a kind of joke,' Fowler told me.

Then he changed the subject. There had been gossip at court that Uncle Thomas was lazy and greedy, and Fowler wanted me to know that it was untrue. Though Thomas was Lord Admiral, it was true that he stayed in court rather than travel with the navy, but that was to look after my interests. There was another thing, Fowler said. The Lord

Admiral was anxious to get married.

'Would Your Grace be pleased if he married?'

'Yes, very well pleased,' I said.

'Who would Your Grace like him to marry?' Fowler went on. I thought carefully. Marriage was a serious business. Uncle Edward's wife was a horrible, stuck-up woman who everybody hated. I wanted better for my favourite uncle.

'My Lady Anne of Cleves,' I suggested first.

To explain about Anne of Cleves, I have to tell you about my father's marriages. When the Pope wouldn't annul his first marriage to Catherine of Aragon (Mary's mother, who could have no more children), my father broke away from the Catholic Church. He formed the Church of England instead, which made it possible for him to divorce his queen. His next wife was Ann Boleyn, Elizabeth's mother. She cheated on him, which is treason. So she was beheaded. Then came my mother, Jane Seymour, who died after having me. Then came Anne of Cleves, a choice he regretted straight away. The marriage was quickly annulled. After Anne came Catherine Howard, who also cheated on him. Beheaded. Finally, my stepmother, Catherine Parr.

I know six marriages seems like a lot but, to my

mind, only two wives count: my mother, whom my father loved (he is buried beside her), and Queen Catherine, who was a kind of replacement and a good stepmother to me and my sisters. Not surprisingly, Elizabeth didn't like to talk about the six wives business. Legally, my sisters were bastards.

I changed my mind about Anne of Cleves. If my father hadn't found her attractive enough seven years ago, my uncle was hardly likely to now.

'No,' I said. 'I would like him to marry my sister Mary, to change her opinions.' Mary, twenty years older than me, was a devout Catholic. Uncle Thomas was a convinced Protestant.

Fowler whispered that he would pass this on and we both went to sleep. But I'd made a terrible mistake. My uncle couldn't marry Mary, I realised, as I tried to drift off. For if I were to die, she would become queen, and he her consort. Whether he meant to or not, Uncle Thomas would, therefore, benefit by my death. For him to marry Mary would be treason.

A few days later, Fowler again brought up the subject of a wife for Uncle Thomas. 'Your uncle wants to know if you would support his being a suitor to Queen Catherine. He will ask if you could write to her on his behalf.'

Since my accession, Queen Catherine, my stepmother, had moved to her own palace in Chelsea, where she had two hundred servants. I missed her. I used to see more of her than I did of my father. Recently, though, she'd had a big row with my uncle Edward and his wife. They wouldn't allow her to keep the crown jewels that came to her when she'd married my father. As Protector, Uncle Edward was always near me, so Catherine didn't visit me often. Elizabeth was staying with her. I was jealous that my sister was still close to our stepmother.

I'd heard the court gossip. People said that Queen Catherine had been in love with my uncle Thomas before my father declared an interest in her. She had now outlived three husbands. At thirty-five, she was still a good-looking woman. If she and Thomas were to marry, I would see more of her, and of Elizabeth. The marriage would also keep my favourite uncle close by.

So I wrote the letter Fowler asked for. I didn't worry what Uncle Edward would make of it. He had enough to do as Protector.

Soon after that, Queen Catherine came to see me.

This great woman, the one I used to call 'mother', now knelt before me.

'Your Grace,' she said to me. 'I need your blessing. You know that I have been attached to Thomas Seymour, the Lord Admiral, for a long time, but that a higher power intervened.'

The 'higher power' was my father, not God.

'Do you wish to marry him?' I asked.

'Sir, I meant to wait two years, but your uncle is a man of such passion...' She hesitated, and I waited for her to finish. 'We were secretly married last week.'

'I see.' My father had only been dead for five months.

6 ✿ Pocket Money

As Protector, Uncle Edward worked long hours. I wasn't invited to Council meetings, so I barely saw him. At times, I felt like I was king in name only. One day Uncle Edward asked to see me on urgent business. He had a face like thunder.

'Your uncle Thomas has secretly married Her Majesty the Queen,' he said.

'He did so with my permission,' I lied.

Uncle Thomas ought not to have married my stepmother so quickly. After all, only five months after the King's death it was possible for the Queen to have been carrying my father's child. She had apologised to me for her hurry. She had explained that this came from her love of Thomas and assured me of her love for me. I'd written my stepmother a letter, supporting her marriage. But we had agreed to keep this secret from Uncle Edward, knowing he would not approve.

John Cheke has told me, more than once, that secrets can soil the soul. However, a king has to keep secrets. They are part of his power, and his burden.

Now the secret was out. Uncle Edward stared at me, waiting for further explanation. He expected me to fill the silence. But a king does not need to explain himself, that was another thing my tutor had told me. So I said nothing more.

Uncle Edward did not conceal his anger. There were thirty years between us. He ought to win any argument. But I was king. Without my support, who was he?

'The Council won't like it,' he said.

'He is your brother. Surely you will defend him.'

'Thomas is my brother but he has his flaws. He is arrogant and greedy and far too attractive to women for his own good.'

'Then best he settle down. He couldn't choose more wisely than Queen Catherine.'

Uncle Edward abruptly changed the subject. We were about to send our armies in to attack Scotland and he wanted me to be engaged to the Scottish queen, Mary, who was only five years old. I'd never met her, but I didn't argue. We talked briefly about the economy, which was in trouble. My father had made millions from selling off land belonging to monasteries, but all that and more had been spent on wars with Scotland and France.

Next, we discussed the Church. Money wasn't all that important to me, but religion was. Religion was about the things that mattered most. Uncle Edward supported me in making Protestantism the religion of England. He was putting our enemies in the Tower. Some people said he was too soft for not executing them. But Uncle Edward was a kind man. I agreed with him: heretics should be given time to change their views, not burnt at the stake. My God was a forgiving God.

At the end of our interview, I brought up the subject of money for my personal use. 'You have everything you need,' Uncle Edward told me. Before I could say more, he claimed that he had urgent business to attend to, and left.

Most of my friends had pocket money. I wanted to be able to treat them. When Barnaby gave me a gift, I wanted the means to give one back. I wanted to be able to reward Fowler, my Gentleman Usher. But I had no pocket money. Uncle Edward said that, as king in a time of financial crisis, I should set an example of economy. But I still needed some money of my own. My uncle Thomas was much more generous with money than Uncle Edward. So, that night, I asked Fowler.

'Is there any way my uncle Thomas can get me more money?'

Fowler said he'd see what he could do.

Soon after, Uncle Thomas visited, handing me two guineas the moment we were alone. 'If Your Grace needs anything,' he said, 'you have only to ask.'

Then we discussed my becoming engaged to the little Scottish queen. The marriage would seal the kingdom into a Great Britain: England, Scotland, Wales and Ireland.

'It will never work,' Thomas told me. 'The Scots will rebel, as they always do. An engagement will only cause you grief. When the time comes for you to marry, there is only one girl I recommend. Your cousin, Lady Jane Grey.'

I knew Jane, a pretty, intelligent girl my own age. She was fifth in line for the throne. Although her parents were living she had recently joined the household of Uncle Thomas and Queen Catherine. But, as King, I would have to marry for political advantage. There was no reason to marry Jane. I thanked my uncle for his advice and asked after his new wife – my stepmother.

'She sends her warmest wishes, Your Grace, as does your sister, Elizabeth.'

He bent my ear about the crown jewels which my stepmother had been given on her marriage to my father. Uncle Edward's wife still refused to let the Queen have them. I had already learnt that it was best to stay out of arguments which did not directly concern me. We agreed that Uncle Edward's wife was a liability. Thomas attacked his brother's meanness.

I defended Uncle Edward. 'The whole country is in terrible debt.'

'But my brother is not. Do you know what land he took when he became Protector? Or how many thousands he's already spent on Somerset House?'

I didn't know. (Somerset House was a palace my uncle was building for himself on The Strand. Two churches had been demolished to make way for it.)

'You know your father never wanted one man to rule the country for you?'

I didn't know that either. But I decided not to take sides in this debate, for I loved both my uncles. And I couldn't ask Uncle Edward for his point of view, because he was away, leading an attack on Scotland.

My best friend, Barnaby Fitzpatrick, was soon going to be a guest at the French Court. I would miss him, and wanted to give him a parting gift. I told Fowler to tell my uncle Thomas that I should like some money now.

Soon after this, Uncle Thomas came himself, unannounced. (Somehow he had managed to have keys made for every room in every palace.) He brought me a huge sum, forty pounds. This allowed me not only to buy Barnaby a new suit of clothes, but also to reward my good tutor, John Cheke, and, of course, Fowler. Both were very grateful.

A few days later, when Parliament was sitting, Uncle Thomas came to see me again. He wanted me to write a letter to the Council about his wife's jewels. I had to think carefully.

'If the cause is good,' I told him, 'the lords of the Council will allow it. If it is ill, I will not write it.' Before he could argue further, I asked him to go. I went at once to see John Cheke, who told me I had done right.

A few more days later, Uncle Thomas was back yet again, full of his usual gusto. He had some advice for me. 'You must take it upon yourself to rule, nephew. For you are wise beyond your years and would rule as well as other kings. Then you may give your men whatever you want.'

I didn't know how to reply. People were always complimenting my intelligence, my maturity. But I was only ten and I needed money. I wanted to be a generous king.

Seeing me hesitate, Uncle Thomas went on. 'My brother is old, and I trust he will not live long.'

'Perhaps it were better he should die,' I said, regretting the words as soon as they were out of my mouth. I was fed up with Uncle Edward, but did not want him dead.

'All you have to do is speak. The Council will listen. You could rule, as other kings do.'

How true was this? I didn't know. I didn't want to know. I wasn't ready.

'I am well enough,' I said, dismissing the idea. Uncle Thomas changed tack. 'My brother keeps you as a beggar king. Who else do you need to give money to?'

It was true. I'd spent the forty pounds he'd given me only two weeks before. There was a long list of people to reward. Not just Cheke and Fowler but a tumbler and a trumpet player and a book binder and many more. I couldn't resist listing them for Uncle Thomas. He promised to reward each one for me. Then he had something else to ask.

'If anything is said against me, don't believe it until I speak to you myself.'

I promised. For I was learning never to believe anything, or anyone.

7 ❀ Trouble

I was soon out of money again. It became all too easy to scribble a note to my uncle Thomas asking for more. Fowler hinted that I should write other letters, too, praising Uncle Thomas as Lord Admiral. I knew what Uncle Thomas wanted. He didn't think it was fair that Uncle Edward, as Protector, had so much power when he, as Lord Admiral, had so little. There was little love left between the two men. Since Uncle Edward wouldn't share power with him, Uncle Thomas meant to take control another way. And he had his supporters, both on and off the Council.

As king, I thought I was above the fray. But one day, at Hampton Court, Uncle Thomas paid me an unexpected visit. He spoke with his usual charm. Even so, I sensed that he was on edge.

In his casual, familiar tone, he told me: 'Your debt to me now stands at over a hundred pounds, but no matter. I need your help. That letter to the Council I mentioned...'

The threat in his words was barely concealed –

the price of my pocket money was his wife getting back her crown jewels. *I should have known*, I thought. Only I was wrong. He wanted much more.

'The time has come. My brother has wasted so much money. He has treated you badly. All you need do is ask the Council to transfer the Protectorship to me.'

He gave me his widest smile. When he was like this, my uncle was impossible to refuse. I told him that what he was suggesting appealed to me.

'Good, good. Here, I have a letter already made out. All you have to do is sign it and I, personally, will take the letter to the Council.'

'But Uncle Edward is away in Scotland. How would it look?'

'I don't care how it *looks*! Do you want me to be Protector or not?'

'Of course I do,' I said, though I was beginning to have doubts. I loved Uncle Thomas dearly, but I made excuses. I said that I really ought to check the wording of the letter with John Cheke.

'Why, the man's a mere schoolmaster,' my uncle complained, though he must have known that John was one of the most educated men in the land.

'I insist,' I said, trying to sound regal as I read the

note before me.

My Lords, it said. *I pray you to favour my Lord Admiral mine uncle's suit.*

I left Uncle Thomas with the impression that I supported him. In a way, I did. But a few words with John Cheke convinced me of my own mind.

'This is far worse than I thought,' he said. 'You must take no more money from him. You must not see him alone. And you must sign nothing.'

'My uncle Thomas shall have no bill signed or written by me,' I promised.

That night Fowler talked of Uncle Thomas in glowing terms. He went on about what a great Protector he would make. Then he told me that Thomas was going to give over his manor, Sudely Castle, to me. The Lord Admiral would not benefit by becoming Protector. But if my uncle was so generous, why was he using a hundred-pound debt to scare me into supporting him? I pretended to sleep, but couldn't. I didn't know where to go for advice. My friend Barnaby was gone. My other uncle was in Scotland. Fowler was Uncle Thomas's man. My stepmother was married to the Lord Admiral. The only person I could talk to was my tutor.

Next day, I tried to bring the matter up with John again.

'Please don't speak of this,' he said.

'But, I need...'

'It is not my place, Your Grace.'

I understood why John didn't want to get further involved. He feared for his position if he meddled in politics. But who else could I turn to? Elizabeth lived with Uncle Thomas. Seeing me on the verge of tears, John spoke softly.

'My duty is to educate you,' he explained. 'I must not overstep the mark.'

John looked away, embarrassed. He knew that he had let me down.

That night, I told Fowler I no longer wished him to sleep in my bedchamber. Only, when I put my head down, I couldn't sleep at all. My dog, Jester, slept in a basket in a corner of the bedchamber. Quietly, so as not to disturb my servants, I crept out of bed. Trying not to wake my pet, I picked up Jester and carried the spaniel back to bed with me.

Jester was no longer a puppy. He was growing far more quickly than I was and was heavy to hold. If only I could become a man as quickly as a puppy became a dog. Then I could tell my uncles what to do, or to hell with them!

Next to me, on the silk sheets, Jester whimpered a little before returning to a deep sleep. There was nothing on his mind beyond being fed in the morning and running around my endless gardens. How I wished I could change places with him!

The warmth of his body and the steady beat of his heart were comforting. Soon, I slept too. But even my dreams were haunted by responsibilities.

8 ❧ The Queen and the Princess

Uncle Edward's Scottish campaign ended in failure. My possible fiancée, the little Queen of Scots, escaped to France, where she was soon engaged to the infant dauphin. In a way, I was relieved. Who wants to be engaged at ten?

As soon as Uncle Edward returned from Scotland, he sent for his brother. Uncle Thomas, I heard, was threatening to make this the blackest Parliament in the history of England. When Edward accused him of neglecting his admiralty duties, Thomas denied it and dared his brother to send him to the Tower.

But they were blood relatives. Soon, the two brothers were friendly again. As for me, after his threatening behaviour, I kept my distance from Uncle Thomas. Then I heard that Queen Catherine was going to have a baby. This was very good news. I thought fatherhood might improve Uncle Thomas's temper.

As Protector, Uncle Edward made only one change that affected me. My beloved tutor, John

Cheke, was banished to Cambridge for taking money from the King (the small gift I had made him a few months earlier). I had lost the one person I could safely confide in. I missed Elizabeth more than ever.

Elizabeth was nearly fifteen, and her life was in turmoil. But nobody told me. What happened next I only found out later (from statements given to the Council by Elizabeth herself and others).

My sister Mary disapproved of Elizabeth staying with Uncle Thomas and Queen Catherine. She wrote inviting Elizabeth to live with her, but Elizabeth liked it where she was and politely refused.

It turned out she liked it too much. One day, when the pregnant Queen visited her stepdaughter's room without warning, she found Elizabeth in her husband's arms. My sister was sent away the next day.

My stepmother gave birth to a healthy baby, called Mary, but died a few days after the birth, just as my own mother had done. So I lost a second mother. The first time, I'd been too young to mourn. This time, I was king, and it would have been unseemly to show distress.

Elizabeth was very ill the following summer. There were rumours that she had miscarried Uncle Thomas's child. The rumours were probably false.

But I cannot be sure. She and I were no longer close. I had nobody close.

At least my relationship with Uncle Edward improved. Now that I was keeping my distance from his brother, it was hard to remember why I'd ever turned against Uncle Edward. That summer, out at Hampton Court, I hunted often. I spent so much time in the company of older boys that I felt and acted older than my eleven years. My companions no longer treated me as a child. In the evening we would put on masques (mostly plays full of revenge, often ending with the death of the Pope!). Or we would play cards. The Bible warned against gambling, but it was excellent sport. I was relieved to be away from the intrigues of Whitehall. Even my stepmother's death did not depress me for long.

One day Uncle Edward visited Hampton Court to discuss affairs of state with me. We were walking in the gallery when, unexpectedly, Uncle Thomas appeared. He had journeyed from London just to see me and seemed put out to find his brother already there.

Uncle Thomas joined us, putting on his oiliest voice. 'Since I saw you last,' he said to me, 'you've grown up to be a good-looking young gentleman.'

I muttered something. It had only been two months since our last, embarrassing encounter, but he looked different too. He was showing his age, and had lost another tooth, disfiguring his smile. Though he was still the Lord Admiral, Uncle Thomas's influence at court was much weakened by Queen Catherine's death. He didn't seem to realise this, or register that things had changed between us. The Lord Admiral carried on talking as though his brother wasn't there.

'I trust that within three or four years, you will be able to rule for yourself. Your Grace will be sixteen years old. I trust by that time Your Grace will be able to support the men that you choose, with such rewards as fall in Your Grace's gift.'

I said nothing, glad that Uncle Edward was there. Uncle Thomas had his maths wrong. It would be more than four years before I was sixteen and I would not be a full king until I was eighteen. Uncle Thomas rambled on, not waiting for me to reply. Maybe he thought that I couldn't speak freely because of his brother. But it was much more than that. I no longer felt comfortable in my uncle Thomas's company. I wanted him to keep away from me.

9 ✿ A Dead Dog

Like all kings, I had my spies. At Whitehall, Uncle Thomas had been overheard telling people how unprotected his nephew was. It would be easy, he'd argued, for him to steal me away and keep me in his house. I'd be happier with him, he said.

There was another disturbing matter. When she was nine, Lady Jane Grey had been sent to live with Queen Catherine to learn manners and social graces. After my stepmother's death, Jane should have left Uncle Thomas's household and returned to her own family. Instead, Uncle Thomas did a thing he'd been planning since my father's death. He bought the guardianship of Lady Jane (still fifth in line for the throne) from her father. Uncle Thomas had always thought that I should marry Lady Jane when we were both older. It was clear what he was playing at.

But there was no advantage to England in my marrying Jane. Uncle Edward would want me to make a marriage which expanded my kingdom. So, even though she lived in France and was engaged to a French prince, the little Scottish queen was still the favourite choice to be my bride.

I was becoming worried about my safety. My sister Mary still attended the Catholic Mass, which Uncle Edward was doing away with. But many people in England were practising Catholics and they were desperate to replace me with a Catholic queen. I could easily be murdered in my bed at Hampton Court. Without telling anyone, I took to locking my inner door at night, leaving Jester in the anteroom between my chamber and the next. That way, if anyone tried to break the door down, Jester's barking would alert me.

One night, not long before I was due to return to Whitehall, I was woken by Jester barking. He never barked needlessly. I sat bolt upright, fear flooding through my body. As I waited, wide-eyed, I heard somebody trying the door. Finding the door locked, whoever it was tried all the harder to open it. Jester barked louder. They had a key, I could hear. It must be one of my men. I feared a fire and ran to the door, meaning to unbolt it. But if it was one of my men, why wasn't he calling to me? Jester barked more fiercely. Then I heard my dog attack whoever was outside. The man in the antechamber swore.

I heard two gunshots. Immediately, there were rapid footsteps beyond the antechamber. Jester didn't bark any more. Shaking, I realised what must have happened. By then, I could hear men running from all over the house, roused by the noise of the gunshots. Finally, through the thick door, I heard the familiar bluster of my uncle Thomas.

'I am here to visit His Grace, the King. Why is his room bolted from the inside? How can this be allowed? Suppose he were to be taken ill? Unhand me!'

When I was sure that he was surrounded, I unbolted the door. My uncle Thomas, gun still in hand, was too distracted to notice my presence. I stood in my nightgown and watched as my yeomen questioned him. At last Thomas gave a mumbled explanation of what he was doing outside my room, in the middle of the night, with a gun in his hand.

'I wished to know whether His Majesty was safely guarded.'

Some of the men seemed to accept this. I did not. At Uncle Thomas's feet, unnoticed, lay my faithful friend Jester. He'd tried to protect me to the end. The dead dog's blood seeped across the stone floor.

I didn't venture out until they had taken Thomas

away. Then I asked one of the yeomen how he had got in. It seems my uncle had climbed a wall and entered through the privy garden gate (for which he had a counterfeit key). Then he had made his way, undisturbed, to my bedchamber.

I don't know what was going on in Thomas's mind. Was he intending to talk to me or to kidnap me? Why did he bring a gun? Did he think, after all that had happened, I would still support him in becoming Protector? Whatever possessed him to make him kill my pet dog? Did he mean to kill me?

I had been a fool to trust him. But he was the bigger fool by far.

I buried Jester in the privy garden, digging the earth myself, damping it down with the first tears I had shed since my father died. Then I ordered that my uncle Thomas, the Lord Admiral, be sent to the Tower.

10 ❧ Traitors

Uncle Edward didn't tell me what was happening at Thomas's trial until it was nearly over. He was protecting me, I suppose. He thought I was still fond of his brother.

The Council heard thirty-five charges against Uncle Thomas. John Dudley, with his intelligent eyes and strong face, led the prosecution. It appeared that, after kidnapping me, Uncle Thomas meant to murder his own brother. Uncle Edward, the Protector, was made to look a fool.

More and more bad things came out about Thomas at the trial. My sister Elizabeth, now fifteen, was questioned for two weeks. She was suspected of plotting to marry Uncle Thomas. She admitted this had been discussed in her house, but insisted that there was never any agreement. There had been rumours that she was pregnant by Thomas. She denied them, adding that she would never have married before my sixteenth birthday or without the Council's permission. But she had to say that. To do otherwise would be treason.

Day after day – all day – they questioned Elizabeth and her servants. My sister was tough. They did not break her. Eventually, they had to send her home.

Uncle Thomas demanded to be tried by jury rather than by the lords of the Council. He thought commoners would be more sympathetic to him. Dudley told Uncle Edward he'd be mad to allow it. As Lord Admiral, Thomas should be tried by other lords. That was when the Council had to put me in the picture. They couldn't act without the King's authority.

The meeting of the Council went on for a very long time. Every member agreed: my uncle Thomas was guilty of treason. I listened carefully to all the evidence. Was Thomas a true traitor? He wanted whatever he could get, but I didn't believe he wanted me dead. Nevertheless, I agreed with the Council. Justice had to be done. I spoke from a complicated script which Uncle Edward had written for me. I tried to learn it by heart but still mucked up a little.

'We do perceive that there is great things objected and laid to my Lord Admiral, mine uncle – and they tend to treason – and we perceive that you require but justice to be done.' I hesitated, for my next words were a death warrant for the uncle I had once loved and admired. 'We think it reasonable – and we will well that you proceed according to your request.'

After I'd spoken, the Council applauded heartily. I was their king and I had done what needed to be done. But Uncle Edward's position as Protector had been undermined. From that point on, when the Council needed to make a decision, many looked first to John Dudley.

A week after the trial, the members of the Council came to me, led by Dudley. The great general spoke to me with passion and humility.

'The Council feels that your uncle Thomas's execution should go ahead without further troubling his brother, the Lord Protector.'

'Why?' I asked, for I did not want to undermine my uncle Edward.

'The Protector is a great man,' Dudley told me. 'Some people think that he is too kind for his own good – his refusal to burn witches, for instance, or to allow death by boiling in oil... some see these as signs of weakness.'

'Is it weak to be kind, or to give heretics a little

time to change their mind?'

'I agree, Your Grace. And I am merely trying to show the same kindness to the Protector. If you would sign this? It would be the work of a moment.'

I took the death warrant from him. Dudley was right. This was my responsibility. What kind of society expects a man to order the execution of his own brother? Then I read the warrant. By law, Thomas should be hung, drawn and quartered: the most horrible of deaths. I could not allow my once favourite uncle to be so tortured. I changed the wording. Then, with steady quill, I signed the warrant and handed it to Dudley.

'I have ordered a simple beheading,' I told him.

'Very good, Your Grace. I'm sure the Council will appreciate the wisdom of your generosity.'

On the eighteenth of March, 1549, the night before his death, Uncle Thomas wrote notes to Elizabeth and Mary, sealing them in his shoe. But he was betrayed by his servants. The notes were found and destroyed. I still wonder what he was thinking. Elizabeth knew Thomas best. *This day,* she wrote to me, *died a man of much wit and little judgment.*

11 ❀ Night Flight

Things were coming to a head. That summer of 1549, when I was nearly twelve, there was rioting and unrest throughout England. There were two main grudges – land ownership and religion, and people felt very strongly about both of them.

For years now, rich landowners had been fencing off common land – land which had once belonged to everybody – for their own private use. No wonder poor people were getting angry. As Protector, my uncle had been raising taxes too. Nobody likes paying more money, especially when they don't have much to begin with. Added to all this, the Catholics of England weren't prepared to accept my religious reforms. They weren't going to give up their old religion without a fight.

When things go wrong, leaders get the blame. As Protector, Uncle Edward was losing popularity fast. After his brother's execution, he always seemed to be in a bad temper. Some blamed his nagging wife. Others blamed the economy, or the disastrous war in Scotland. Members of the Council complained that

Uncle Edward never listened to advice. Worse, he kept changing his mind. One month he'd make new laws about religious reform or land rents. The next month he'd overturn them.

Dudley could see which way the wind was blowing, but I couldn't. I wasn't ready for any of it.

The first uprising against us was in Cornwall. Soon, landowners were under siege in Oxfordshire and Buckinghamshire. I had been king for less than eighteen months.

Next, my sister Mary's Catholic supporters started riots in Norwich, only twenty miles from her house. Exeter and Norwich were soon taken by the rebels.

My armies took back the towns. However, a rebel army, three thousand strong, remained just outside Norwich. John Dudley led the army against them. I daydreamed of being by his side, of proving myself as a warrior, like my father. And I waited.

It was September before Dudley returned to London, victorious. His men had destroyed the rebel army, mercilessly slaughtering every single man. We should all have been celebrating, but while Dudley went to meet the Council, Uncle Edward rode out in the opposite direction to visit me in

Hampton Court. And he brought five hundred troops with him.

'I have sent for Dudley,' he told me. 'We have matters to sort out.'

I didn't understand why my uncle couldn't see Dudley in London. Still, I looked forward to the great general's arrival. His success with the rebels was all the more welcome because of my uncle's failures in Scotland.

But Dudley stayed in London. My uncle dictated a letter to the Council, demanding Dudley's presence. I had no choice but to sign it. After that was done, Uncle Edward paced the long corridors of Hampton Court, waiting for Dudley to arrive. Time crept by. It was a relief to leave him that night, go to my bed. But I had no sooner gone to sleep than my servants awoke me. Uncle Edward marched into my bed chamber, his face pinched with anger.

'We have to go to Windsor,' he said. 'You'll be safer there.'

'Safe from whom?' I asked. Windsor Castle was in a forest. Once its gates were locked behind me, it would be the devil's own job for an enemy to get in.

'I'll explain on the way,' Uncle Edward said. 'We must leave at once.'

I wasn't happy to be treated this way. Only my uncle could get away with it. I wondered, not for the first time, how we would get on when I came of age, in six years' time. Then, uncle or no uncle, I would be fully in charge. I didn't think he'd like it.

'What's going on?' I asked Uncle Edward as my valet packed some clothes.

'A conspiracy,' he told me. 'Our support in the Council is falling away.'

Did he mean *my* support, or *his*? My uncle seemed to think of himself as in charge. Wasn't I the King? Or was I a mere pawn? On that very day, I discovered later, the members of the Council had set out for Hampton Court to see me, but my uncle had sent them a warning – if they tried to take me, he would have them arrested as traitors. So except for four men, they stayed away. Archbishop Cranmer and three other members of the Council carried on to join us. That was all the support my uncle had left.

'They mean to kill me,' he said, as we hurried out of the palace.

I made no reply. I'd always thought of the Council as *they*. It scared me that now my uncle did, too. But I was distracted. It was bitterly cold when we left, yet, waiting in the Base Court, there was a huge crowd. Trumpeters announced my arrival. We crossed the moat, which was newly filled. Uncle Edward urged me to step forward. I took a deep breath and raised my hand.

'Good people,' I said, 'I pray you to be good to us – and to our uncle.'

The crowd cheered. My uncle stepped forward and took my hand. When the crowd calmed a little, he made a speech.

'I shall not fall alone. If I am destroyed, the King will be destroyed. Kingdom, commonwealth – all will be destroyed together.' Then, to my surprise, he pulled me forward. 'It is not I they shoot at,' he shouted. *This is the mark they shoot at!'*

That said, he led me into the courtyard, where we mounted our horses. As we rode out, I waved the jewelled dagger that my father had given me. The crowd cheered. I wanted to speak to them but Uncle Edward made us hurry on.

Our small party rode through the night. The autumnal air sent chills right through me. The journey was long and I wasn't looking forward to arriving. Windsor was a drab, uncomfortable castle. I didn't care to spend long there.

My uncle and I said little to each other as we rode.

We were the same blood. He took my loyalty for granted. I believed him when he said we were both in danger. Yet this was worse than when Uncle Thomas had tried to break into my room. Then, the danger quickly passed. Only my dog had died. But now, if all the Council were against me, anything could happen. I might meet the same fate as Thomas. My sister Mary might be queen by the end of the week. Catholics across the land would rejoice. And my reforms would be over before they'd really begun.

We rode through the cold, windy night, arriving just before dawn. I went inside. The shabby castle was chilly and ill prepared for a visit. After I'd eaten a cold breakfast, there was a great commotion outside. When I went to look, there were three hundred men waiting. Archbishop Cranmer was at the front, having brought most of the men from Hampton Court. His long white beard (which he never cut in memory of my father) twisted in the chill wind.

'What do you do here at such an hour?' I asked the Archbishop.

'Sir, suffice it that we are here,' he replied.

I knew then that they were there to defend the castle from a siege.

12 ❧ John Dudley

I tried to sleep but dozed only briefly. I dreamt that Dudley was at the gates of Windsor Castle, ordering me to return to London. John Dudley, the Earl of Warwick, had been a renowned general during my father's reign. During the recent uprisings, he had proved himself to be the greatest general we had. Even so, some people didn't like him. They said he was too cagey, that he weighed up every situation until he saw how he could take advantage. But that was the way everybody behaved at court. Except for me. I was king by divine right. I had no need to manipulate others.

John Dudley was born a commoner, the son of one of my father's lawyers. He had risen far. He was a Protestant who stayed friendly with the Catholics at court. Unlike Uncle Edward, John Dudley was a politician.

The next morning I woke to find I had a cough. I'd caught a chill during the ride. Normally, when I was ill, everyone fussed over me. Any person with the slightest illness was kept away. The best doctors were called for. That day, though, there were higher priorities. I wrapped up warm and concealed my discomfort.

Messengers sped between London and Windsor all day. My cold got worse. I began to feel I was in prison. I was a king, destined to live in the lap of luxury. I took the gardens and galleries of Hampton Court for granted. Windsor Castle was bleak, draughty. I did not want to die in a place like this.

Archbishop Cranmer tried to persuade my uncle to go to London, to negotiate. Nobody wanted a civil war and maybe he could prevent it. But Uncle Edward was proud, and wary. While he had me, he had power. We shared the same family blood. I could not desert him. I didn't know what he'd do if I tried to. That night, he asked me to write to the Council. I stayed up late, coughing and spluttering, trying to decide what to put.

I needn't have bothered. In the morning, my uncle dictated the words I must use to defend him before the Council: *Each man hath his faults, he his and you yours... he meaneth us no hurt... He is our Uncle, whom you know we love... Proceed not to extremities against him.* My uncle added his own assurances of good behaviour. I wished he had let me write my own letter. If they recognised my genuine voice, the members of the Council might do as I asked. But the letter was sent off with a messenger. We waited anxiously for a response.

The reply was a long time in coming. When it did arrive, the letter was written by John Dudley and delivered by Sir Philip Hoby. In it the Council begged the Protector not to frighten me and promised to treat him fairly. This letter, I later discovered, had already been read out to the crowds in London. The people supported Dudley. And why shouldn't they? Uncle Edward's time as Protector had not been a success. We had lost the war in Scotland. Prices had gone up by three times since my father's reign.

Sir Philip Hoby told my uncle that he could keep his freedom and most of his lands if he surrendered the Protectorship.

My cold, meanwhile, was no better. I sweated, shivered and sneezed.

Two days later Sir Philip returned with a written promise from the lords of the Council. If my uncle submitted to arrest, he could keep his honours and his property. This was read out to me, in Uncle Edward's presence. When he had finished, Hoby turned to me.

'My Lord,' he said, 'don't be afraid. If you should come to any harm, I will lose this.' He was pointing at his neck. Then he pledged his loyalty to me.

My uncle withdrew into himself. He was angry and shaken. It was hard to know what he was thinking. He certainly didn't confide in me. If he was worried about my health, he didn't show it. Finally, he said to Sir Philip, 'I will receive their lordships tomorrow.'

He stamped out of the room and I had to spend my third night in the castle, coughing and sweating and fearing for my life.

When I woke the next morning, my cold had mysteriously vanished. The lords of the Council had already arrived from London for breakfast at Windsor. After meeting my uncle, they lined up to kiss my hand. The Protector, they told me, had agreed to be placed under guard.

There followed a long meeting in which the members of the Council told me what was going on. There were many charges against my uncle, most of them to do with theft. He had, for instance, kept the thousand gold crowns that the City of London had given me on the day of my coronation. According to the Council, Uncle Edward had made himself rich while he kept me short of money. I still found it hard to believe that my wise, religious uncle was such a hypocrite. His greatest offence was the flight to Windsor which had made me ill. Putting the King's life at risk was a serious crime. Uncle Edward was to be imprisoned in the Tower.

13 🌸 King at Last

I didn't visit Uncle Edward in the Tower. Dudley persuaded me not to go. Instead, I promised my uncle mercy. When I told this to the Council, they seemed unsure of what to do. Dudley stood up and addressed them passionately. 'My lords, we must return good for evil. It is the King's will that his uncle should be pardoned, and it is the first matter he has asked of us. We ought to accede to His Grace's wishes.'

Nobody spoke against him. Everything, I realised, had changed. From that meeting on, I felt as though I was finally, truly king.

On October 12th it was my twelfth birthday. Dudley came to see me. He wished me a happy birthday and then told me what was going on.

'The Council has agreed there is no need to replace the Protector.'

'Surely, with so many on the Council, you still need a leader?' It was as clear to me as it was to everyone else that Dudley had assumed that role.

'Yes, but your father's will did not mention the

need for a Protector. The Council has elected me as their president. I am happy to serve you in every way possible. But I say to you, Your Grace, in my view, you are as much king at twelve as you will be at twenty or forty. Your divine powers flow from your majesty, not from your age. You are the law, only answerable to our Lord God.'

I acknowledged this statement with a dismissive bow, remembering that Uncle Edward had once said something similar, then kept power to himself. Inwardly, though, I was pleased. When Dudley asked if there was anything he could do for me, I at once mentioned money. He told me that I could have as much as I wanted.

'I would also like the return of my tutor, John Cheke, from Cambridge.'

'He's a fine man,' Dudley said. 'The university will be unhappy to lose him, but I shall send for him at once.'

He then begged permission to visit me at Hampton Court.

In a matter of days, it seemed, everything was sorted out to my satisfaction. Dudley made it clear that he supported my religious views. He even read a short book about religion which I'd written for my uncle the year before. My uncle had never got round to looking at it. Dudley had it published.

There were twenty-nine charges against Uncle Edward. Most concerned the theft of money or land. He admitted all the crimes and appealed for mercy. We fined him £2,000. This punishment, combined with the loss of the Protectorship, seemed enough. He was released from the Tower and told to live as a private man, keeping himself always at least ten miles from the King's person. Two months later, he was allowed to return to court. His lands were restored and he was invited to eat dinner at my table.

Imprisonment had changed my uncle. His beard was greyer and his face was sallow, but it was more than that. His arrogance had gone. So had his passion. He was a defeated man.

In recognition of his great work as President of the Council, I decided to make Dudley, already Earl of Warwick, the Duke of Northumberland. He comes to see me often. We practise archery together and he consults me on every aspect of running the kingdom. Uncle Edward left the economy in a terrible mess, but at least the uprisings are over. John Dudley supports my religious reforms. He's keeping a close eye on my sister Mary. When we meet, I argue with her, but in a friendly fashion. She says she's too old to change her religion. We agree to disagree. This is easier for me than it is for her. In the end, to win the argument, all I have to do is stay alive. As long as I am king, Protestantism will remain the country's official religion.

The other day, John Cheke suggested that I keep some kind of journal, a chronicle of my reign. I must not include my thoughts and feelings, only what happens. Even so, the act of writing things down makes me think about them in greater depth. I will have to choose my words more carefully than I have here. A king must not show fear or favour. So I end this account, with the country in good hands and my own spirits higher than they have ever been before.

Part Two: 1553

14 🎀 Royal Progress

I am fifteen. At night I sleep in the bed my father died in. Curiously, it is a kind of comfort. Doctors come and go, never telling me what they think. It is treason to predict the death of a king. Even to cast my horoscope could cost the astrologer his life. But you don't need to be an astrologer to guess my future.

I kept the journal for two and a bit years, but I've given the thing up now. It was a waste of time, a schoolboy exercise. In it, I recorded the battles, religious reforms, even my engagement (to a French princess I never met), the masques and tournaments, the parades and the speeches I made. I would write down what happened, only what happened. Like this, written at the beginning of the year: *The Duke of Somerset had his head cut off upon Tower Hill between eight and nine o'clock in the morning.*

That's right. Both of my uncles are dead now. Uncle Edward died with more dignity than his brother. People cried outside the Tower. They say he was plotting against John Dudley: my uncle wanted to set up a coup to defeat Dudley, who'd done the same thing to him. The way I saw it, either man could dominate the Council on his own, but they couldn't work together. So one of them had to go. Dudley, being the more ruthless, struck first.

It's odd. My uncle became more popular after he stopped being Protector. The crowds cheered him before his execution. When a rumour spread that he'd been reprieved, there was dancing in the streets. Nobody believed the charges against him. Maybe his coup would have succeeded, if he hadn't had his head chopped off first.

Now nobody trusts Dudley. They say that, for everything he does, he has at least four reasons. He's too clever for his own good. I think he's been unlucky. It's the weather, you see. Under Uncle Edward, there were uprisings, but we had good harvests. Since Dudley took over, we've had nothing but rain. There was an epidemic of sweating sickness, too. Thousands died. John Cheke was nearly one of them. We've had no uprisings, only small riots. People are too sick to rebel.

I feel cheated. Haven't I been a good little king? So healthy, so clever. So interested in religion, they talk about me becoming a saint. I'd have settled for becoming as good a king as my father. Just this spring, Dudley had Parliament bring forward the date of my majority. I will become all-powerful king next year, on my sixteenth, rather than my eighteenth birthday. I don't know if I'll last that long.

It was the Royal Progress that did me in. Dudley's idea was for me to travel across the southern counties of the kingdom, staying in grand houses on the way. I would seal my popularity in the country and strengthen my alliances with the great families of my kingdom. At first, I enjoyed myself. But soon there was too much to do, too many people who wanted a piece of my time. I got fed up of making speeches, opening shipyards, crowds full of people wanting to touch me.

In August, after two months on tour, I was pale and ill. I thought I'd made a good recovery from the measles earlier in the year. The doctors insisted it was only exhaustion. We cancelled the rest of the tour, blaming lack of money. I stopped at Windsor, too ill to travel further. An Italian doctor told me all I needed was rest.

But then there were many disputes over my second prayer book, which occupied much of my energy. Christmas and New Year passed peacefully enough, but now I feel worn out.

I was plump as a child and hated it. I grew to loathe my fat-faced portrait. Over the last two years I have grown lean. My voice and face have become manly. But now my cheeks swell again, as does my belly. My image in a mirror sickens me. It is not fat, for I scarcely eat. There are other symptoms. I have a cough I can't get rid of. I spit blood. I have a sickness. The doctors won't tell me what it is.

The Council think all I care about these days is religion, but I keep my ear to the ground. Dudley has started acting friendly to my sister, Mary. He's sent her money and authorised repairs to her estates. That can only mean one thing.

15 ✿ Succession

Forgive me if I make no sense, or repeat myself. I'm feverish. At the beginning of February, I took walks in the park and felt my health slowly recover. Then March approached and I felt worse than before. The month was set aside for a special Parliament to raise much needed money. I was too ill to travel to Westminster, so I opened the Parliament at Whitehall instead. This month, April, I came by water to my palace at Greenwich. As I left Whitehall there were loud gun salutes, both from the Tower and from three large ships, about to set off for Newfoundland. The noise made my head ache and I did not enjoy the journey as I usually do.

I have to put my house in order. I want to see my sister Elizabeth. She's the one. She will be queen if I die young. Mary has always been in poor health. She won't last. So Elizabeth will succeed. Unless Mary kills her. Which she might. There's no love lost there. But Elizabeth knows how to play the game. Since her time living with Uncle Thomas and my stepmother, she has behaved impeccably, a true

Protestant princess. Yet if I die, and Mary becomes queen, Elizabeth would convert to Catholicism, just to please her. She's no fool.

What if Mary manages to marry, though, have a child? She's thirty-six, an old and ugly thing. But a queen is a queen. Some mighty men will be interested. Catholic men. Queen Catherine, my stepmother, had a baby at thirty-five, though it killed her. If Mary has a child ... then the whole thing would go down the drain. If only I was old enough to marry and father a child. Bring me that clever girl, Lady Jane, the one my uncle Thomas wanted me to have. You were right, uncle! She'll do. Sorry, you're dead, aren't you? I'll see you soon, Uncle Thomas, pay back that money I owe you.

The old witch came to see me. They kept her waiting for three days but, in the end, they had to let her in. Hard to believe we were so close when I was a little boy. Last time I saw my sister Mary, I spent a couple of hours trying to persuade her to convert. She said that she was too old for a new religion. In the end we had to agree to disagree. Which is rubbish. Because we both know that, in this world, all that matters is how you prepare for the next world. Everything else is vanity.

Mary was shocked when she saw me. Didn't even try to hide it. She wouldn't get close, afraid of infection I suppose. I was too weak to say much. I coughed a lot and spat blood. She didn't stay long. As soon as she'd gone, I cancelled the child masque which we'd planned for that night. Better to send the little mites home than let them catch a killing cold from their king.

Why should my bastard sister become queen? The tide of history is with me, and people are slowly changing. Many towns are setting up grammar schools. They want their children to be able to read and write. They name the schools after me. When the young can read for themselves, they will learn to love and obey the true religion. That's all I care about, the religion that my father began but which Mary wants to destroy.

At times I feel better and go for short walks outdoors. There are no games now, no sport. I read and pray. I wish they would tell me what is wrong with me.

16 🎗 The King's Device

It's summer. Time is running out. In the city, rumours spread that I am dead already. Dudley makes me appear at a window of the palace so that the crowd can see me. I wave feebly, feeling as though I'm in a masque. The well wishers cheer half-heartedly, then go away.

Dudley asks my permission for his son, Guildford, to marry the Lady Jane Grey. I give it, warmly. He is plotting something, I know that. After the marriage, the couple do not live together. I can see what is going on. It will be easy to get Lady Jane's marriage annulled if she has not shared a marriage bed with Guildford.

No marriage bed for me now. That's one pleasure I will never know. The only feeling I have is in my stomach. The blood I cough up is purple-black and reeks so badly it would make those sick who smell it. I can't sleep unless they pump me full of opiates to kill the pain. Nights merge with the days. Only one thought possesses me now, obsesses me. I must stop Mary from becoming queen.

Dudley brings me a woman doctor. Who has heard of such a thing? The medicine she gives me is potent and painful. She looks strange – small and round – but she insists that she can save my life. I'm sure that she's a quack. Why, the medicine she gives me hurts even more than my disease. But I linger on. I should be dead by now. My nails are falling out. So is my hair. My skin flakes in all the places where it isn't covered in scabs. My eyes are bloodshot, hollow.

I send for Dudley. When he comes, I am screaming with pain. He asks the quack to give me more drugs. I say no. I want to be able to think clearly.

'I am not going to live to see sixteen, you must realise that.'

'I fear it, Your Grace,' Dudley replies.

'I want to make a will.'

'You cannot make a will before you're sixteen, Your Grace. The law regards you as a child.'

Groaning, I begin to lift myself up. Dudley, concealing his distaste, reaches forward to help me. I spit the words which seal our fate.

'I am the law. You ... are my instrument. If I will it, so it shall be.'

'The Council...' Dudley begins, but I interrupt.

'The Council will do what I tell them to do.'

'I don't know if that's true, Your Grace,' Dudley whispers.

'Then we'd better find out,' I reply. 'Tell them I wish to disinherit the Lady Mary. My sister Elizabeth must become queen after I die. She will carry on what I have started.'

'It won't work,' Dudley tells me me. 'If you disinherit Mary, you must disinherit Elizabeth too. They are both bastards.'

We argue the toss for some time, until I am tired and can see no way around it. In truth, I'm not sure that Elizabeth will accept the throne if I disinherit Mary. For, if Mary fights back, and wins, she will have Elizabeth's head.

'Very well then,' I say. 'My father's sister, the Lady Jane's mother, is next in line.'

'She can be persuaded to relinquish her claim in favour of her daughter.'

'Get it done.'

When Dudley returns, a day later, I'm having a nightmare. My father, bloated and old, invites me to share his grave. Dudley is standing by me when I wake.

'It is done. The time has come for you to write a will.'

Together, we work on the wording. Even so, when I write it down, I make a mistake about whose children follow who. Too tired to start again, I write a correction above.

'You think your son will make a good king?' I tease Dudley.

'King Consort,' Dudley corrects me. 'The Lady Jane would become queen if...'

'Consort or no, you will rule. You will make sure my work carries on.'

'Oh yes, Your Grace.'

'Better send Guildford to share his marriage bed,' I mutter.

'It is done, Your Grace,' Dudley replies. I imagine the dull, oafish Guildford with the clever, sensitive Jane and I retch, spraying the bed clothes with purple sputum.

'Have the papers drawn up,' I order.

The rest is detail. Some members of the Council protest about my device to deprive Mary of the throne. There are arguments, even talk of treason.

'I won't let them stand in your way,' Dudley tells me. 'I have offered to fight in my shirt sleeves any man who dares challenge your will.'

'Send the Council to see me now,' I instruct him, and they come, man after man, to see me on my death bed. I ask each to sign a document, supporting my new will. If they argue or show signs of doubt, I fix them with a stare of such holy desperation, they cave in. Archbishop Cranmer asks if he might consult a judge before signing (he's worried about committing treason). He is my godfather so I let him, for which he is grateful. John Cheke, now a Council member, is harder to convince.

'I do not trust a god whose true religion disinherits orphans,' he says. But in the end, he, too signs. Most agree willingly, for they love me. And who can deny such a holy king, in such agony, his dying wish?

Dudley sends away the quack. Rumours spread that he is poisoning me. Dudley is the sort of man about whom there will always be rumours. There are fresh rumours that I have died. One night a huge crowd gathers at Greenwich, hearing that I would show myself. But I can't get out of bed. The next night they come again, but are told that the air is too chilly for me to appear. It's July, but my bones feel as cold as the grave.

I'm sorry, Elizabeth, sorry it couldn't be you.

The end must be near now. Men gather in my room. I can barely make out their faces. The doctor asks what I am doing and I tell him that I was praying to God. Where are my friends? Come closer. Hold me.

'I am faint. Lord have mercy on me and take my spirit.'

Afterword

King Edward VI died on July 6th, 1553, aged fifteen. The cause of his death is not clear and will never be known, because his body has been lost. The best guess is that he died of tuberculosis. His pain was probably made worse by the doses of arsenic which a woman 'doctor' gave him to prolong his life. The use of arsenic led to accusations that the King was poisoned by John Dudley.

Lady Jane Grey was not aware of Dudley's plot. Reluctantly, she allowed herself to be pronounced queen. But she refused to name her husband, Guildford Dudley, as king consort. Edward's will, however, was fated from the start. While his father – a powerful and popular king – could get away with changing the law to ensure the succession he wanted, Edward could not. He was seen by many as Dudley's puppet (ironically, the final conspiracy was undoubtedly Edward's idea). Queen Jane had little popular support. There were no public celebrations on her accession to the throne. Mary gathered an army about her, and town after town declared her queen.

Queen Jane sent Dudley – now tired, old and very unpopular – to lead an army against Mary. By the time that his army got close to hers, most of his men had deserted. Nearly all of the lords of the Council had defected to Mary. For the first time in British history, public opinion had affected the future of the monarchy.

Queen Jane returned her crown jewels and was sent to the Tower. She was spared at first, but eventually executed (at a time when an example was needed). Queen Mary arrived in London to huge celebration. She forgave most of those who had opposed her, but this did not include Dudley, who was beheaded. As he was led to his execution, Dudley confessed that all of the charges against the former Protector, Edward Seymour, were completely false.

Mary's bloody reign was even shorter than Edward's. She married Philip of Spain, but had no children. Many Protestant 'heretics' were burnt, but she did not have time to reverse the reformation. Edward's reforms were carried on by his sister, Elizabeth I, who became the most famous queen in Britain's history.

Acknowledgements and Further Reading

Edward VI doesn't come over well in many history books. I was surprised by how often historians contradicted each other (particularly on the cause of his death). Many paint Edward as an unpleasant character – a rather raw deal for somebody who lived his life under enormous pressures and died so young. Books aimed at children are worse, often suggesting that Edward was a sickly child, whose death was inevitable. Until April 1552, this was far from true. I hope that the novel you've just read has corrected some common mistakes without adding new ones.

In Part One, I often used real dialogue drawn from contemporary sources, with only occasional compressions and simplifications. In Part Two, I was forced to invent much more, but Edward's dying words are his. I'm particularly indebted to *The Last Tudor King* by Hester W. Chapman (1958, Jonathan Cape, out of print). Also to *Edward VI* by Jennifer Loach (1999, Yale English Monarch series) and *Edward VI: The Threshold of Power*, *Edward VI: The Young King*, both by W. K. Jordan (1968 and 1970, George Allen & Unwin Ltd, out of print).

The best readily available book about the period between Henry VIII's death and Elizabeth I's accession to the throne is Alison Weir's *Children of England* (1996, Pimlico). This covers the lives of Edward, Mary, Elizabeth and Lady Jane Grey and is a good read. I would like to thank the staff of Nottingham City Libraries for helping me to locate and allowing me to endlessly renew most of the books mentioned above. You can have them back now.

David Belbin

Glossary

Ambassador
An official of the highest rank sent by one country as its long term representative to another country

Antechamber
A small room leading into a larger room and often used as a waiting room

Bill
A written proposal for a new law

Clergy
The collective name for people ordained for religious service

Consort
The husband or wife of a reigning monarch

Coronation
The ceremony of crowning a monarch

Courtier
An aristocrat who attends a king or queen

Dauphin
Heir to the French throne

Devout
Very religious

Epidemic
Fast spreading disease

Hypocrite	A person who pretends to have admirable principles but behaves otherwise
Joust	Medieval tournament
Majority	Age of legal responsibility
Masque	A dramatic entertainment in which the performers wore masks
Realm	Kingdom
Revellers	Merrymaker
Suffice	Enough
Yeoman	Attendant to nobility or royalty